The Emperor and the Nightingale

C30 026 639

Illustrations by Kwan Shan Mei

Story by Helen East

(retold from an original by Chia Hearn Chek)

Macdonald

Long ago, the Emperor of China
had a beautiful garden
full of birds.
All day
they sang in the garden,
and the Emperor listened
in his palace.
But when night came
the birds stopped singing,
and the Emperor closed
the palace doors.
So he never heard
the nightingale,
singing alone
in the dark.

Many people came to the palace
from all round the world,
to talk to the Emperor
and to listen to the birds.
Loveliest of all
of the sounds that they heard
was the song of the nightingale,
the smallest, dullest bird.

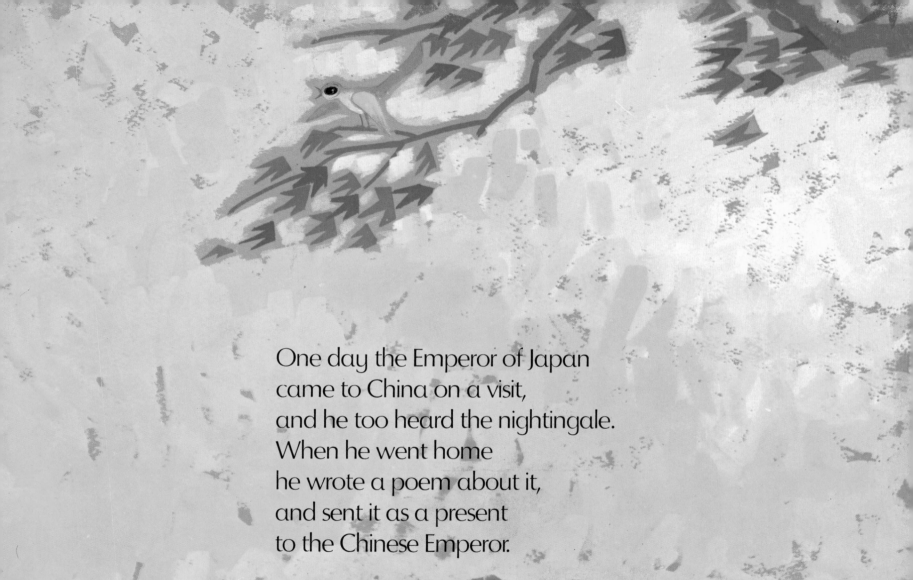

One day the Emperor of Japan
came to China on a visit,
and he too heard the nightingale.
When he went home
he wrote a poem about it,
and sent it as a present
to the Chinese Emperor.

The Emperor of China
read the poem with surprise.
He too loved
the singing of the birds.
But he had never heard
the sweetest song of all.
The shy bird,
who sang at night.
The nightingale.
"Bring me this bird at once!"
the Emperor cried.

All day everyone searched for the bird,
but no-one saw her until night fell.
Then the Emperor's daughters
heard her sing,
and saw her sitting all alone
in a willow tree.
They whistled to her softly
and she whistled back to them.
They threw open the palace doors
and the nightingale flew in.

The nightingale
flew straight to the Emperor.
"Sing!" he commanded,
and the nightingale sang.
Her song was sweeter
to the Emperor
than any other sound
he had ever heard.
"The nightingale
must stay with me for ever,
and sing for me every night!"
the Emperor cried.

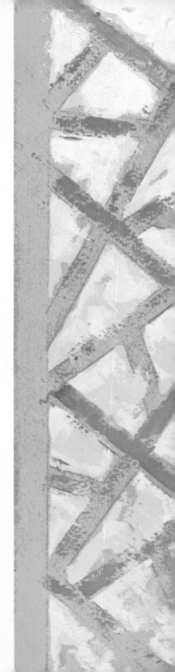

But a few months later,
the Emperor of Japan
sent another present
to the Emperor of China.
It was a golden clockwork toy
shaped like a nightingale.
It could sing and dance
so cleverly,
the Emperor was delighted.
He played with it all the time.
He forgot the real nightingale.

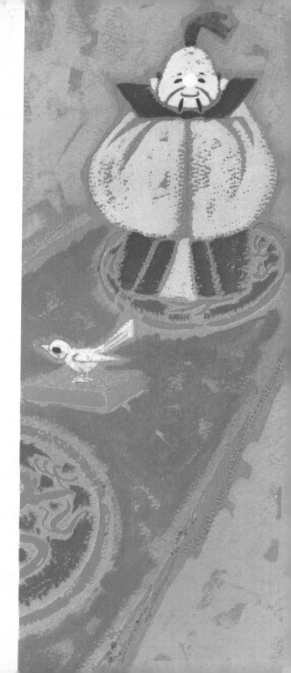

No-one listened to the nightingale now.
No-one saw her sadly flying away.

But one day the toy bird
suddenly stopped singing.
"Sing!" commanded the Emperor,
but the bird could not.
It had broken inside.

All the craftsmen in China
were called to the palace,
to mend the toy bird.
But they could not.
The bird was broken for ever.

Then at last the Emperor
remembered the real nightingale.
"Bring back that bird at once!" he said.
Everyone ran out into the garden
and searched high and low.
But the nightingale had gone.

The Emperor was most unhappy.
He longed to hear the nightingale.
He could not eat.
He could not sleep.
Before long he was ill.
All the doctors in China
were called to the palace
to cure him.
But none of them could help him.

Day by day
the Emperor grew worse.
Soon it was clear that
he was dying.
The palace was quiet.
The people were crying.

The Emperor was lying
alone in the dark.
Then suddenly he heard
the soft notes of the nightingale.
Sitting at his window.
Singing in the night.

Tears rolled down the Emperor's cheeks,
as he heard the song
of the nightingale.
He struggled to sit up
and to welcome the bird.
"Thank you nightingale," he said.

The Emperor grew well again.
But he never forgot the nightingale.
All day long
the birds sang in his garden,
and the Emperor listened
in his palace.
But every night
he went out by himself,
to listen to the nightingale
singing alone in the dark.